ADVENTURES OF A SLIME

BOOKS KID

Silver Dolphin Books
An imprint of Printers Row Publishing Group
A division of Readerlink Distribution Services, LLC
10350 Barnes Canyon Road, Suite 100, San Diego, CA 92121
www.silverdolphinbooks.com

All notations of errors or omissions should be addressed to Silver Dolphin Books, Editorial
Department, at the above address. All other correspondence (author inquiries, permissions)
concerning the content of this book should be addressed to:
404 éditions
c/o Édi8
12 avenue d'Italie
75013 Paris, France
www.lisez.com/404-editions/24

ISBN: 978-1-68412-921-8
Manufactured, printed, and assembled in Crawfordsville, Indiana, U.S.A.
Second printing, April 2020. LSC/04/20
24 23 22 21 20 2 3 4 5 6

ADVENTURES OF A
SLIME

Slibertius, the slime who wants to be a fashion designer!

Written by Books Kid
Introduction by Aypierre
Translated from the French by Daria Chernysheva
Illustrated by Elliot Gaudard

Silver Dolphin

INTRODUCTION FROM AYPIERRE

Slime... Rarely has an enemy been so well named.

This gelatinous, bouncing mass has, over time, however, become one of the best-known monsters in the world of video games.

Everything began in 1986 with a famous Japanese role-playing game, *Dragon Quest*, when a slime became the game's mascot. After slime characters appeared in other more or less popular games (including *Slime Rancher* and *Slime-san*), it became obvious that Minecraft was going to have to have its own version of a slime monster.

Minecraft's slimes are elusive and mysterious creatures. Inhabitants of the deep, slimes are found in the darkest and most secluded caves in the world. As a result, not much is known about the slime's way of life...So, I grabbed my explorer's helmet and my spelunking equipment, I armed myself with my trusty pickax, and I set out to explore these dangerous underground spaces filled with deadly traps and bloodthirsty creatures. After encountering many dangers, I was able to reach the deepest caves, where sunlight never shines.

It took me a few minutes to finally notice them. It's quite a sight: you've got to see these strange, slimy monsters without arms or legs jumping in every direction.

AND WHAT A NUISANCE TO FIGHT!

In fact, a slime has a curious defense mechanism: it has an annoying habit of dividing when you strike it, creating miniature copies of itself.

Though tiny, these little horrors are not to be taken lightly! I found myself pushed into lava by waves of mini slimes more times than I care to remember.

The problem with slimes is that, despite everything, they are very useful when building things with redstone.

A little bit of slime residue, correctly used, can work wonders in creating: automatic doors, flying machines, mechanisms for launching torpedoes...I've lost count of the times when a difficult problem was solved with a few well-placed blocks of slime or sticky pistons.

To be honest, I even ended up creating my own slime farm, so that I wouldn't have to place myself in danger by hunting for slimes.

So, imagine my surprise when I discovered the adventures of Slibertius! Before reading his story, I was far from imagining that a Minecraft slime could have any ambition other than being used to complete a redstone machine circuit. But, in thinking about it, I suppose it's not everyone's greatest dream to end up as a block or a piston...

But fashion designer—that is a surprise! I believe I ought to wish you the best of luck, Slibertius. You're going to need it if you're going to break into the world of fashion (without arms or legs)!

DAY 1

I SAW MY REFLECTION IN THE WATER OF THE SWAMP AND SIGHED.

Im Slibertius, but everyone calls me Bert. And Im a slime. I hate being a slime.

Would you like being a slime?

We're all sticky and gooey and don't have a proper shape. We're nothing but a block of, well, slime.

AND YOU CAN'T DO MUCH WHEN YOU'RE NOTHING BUT A PILE OF JELL-O.

Grumbling, I forced myself to look away from my reflection. It was too depressing. If only I were a skeleton, a zombie, or a witch. Heck, even being a cow or a pig would be more fun than being a slime. At least they have four legs. They can walk, run, or gallop. While I...I have to get around by jumping.

JUMPING!

It's humiliating.
As I hopped from place to place in search of Minecraftians to snack on, I made up little rhymes in my head to make my bouncing a little more fun.

Hop on a log,
Turn into a dog!
Hop on a leaf,
Turn into a thief!
Hop on a tree,
Turn into a bee!
Hop on some grass,
Fall flat on your back!

I tried to come up with something better for that last one, but I couldn't, so I stopped. Besides, I'd just caught a whiff of something interesting.

MINECRAFTIANS!

There's nothing like sinking your teeth into a nice, juicy Minecraftian to make you feel better! And, if my sense of smell wasn't wrong—and it never was—there were three, sitting around a campfire, as ripe as can be.

I let my nose guide me—what's that? You didn't think that slimes had noses? Well, we do. It's just that the nose is very oozy, so it melts in with all our other ooziness. It's an important part of our camouflage. Anyway, as I was saying, I let my nose guide me, and I soon spotted the flickering campfire.

"A SLIME! DRAW YOUR SWORDS!"

Seeing me approach, the panicked humans scattered, and I chose one to pursue. I jumped with all my might and landed right beside him. He was so frightened he dropped his weapon!

His friends tried to create a distraction, but, once a slime has chosen his prey, nothing can make him change his mind—and this Minecraftian was in no shape to fight against my supreme power.

Soon enough, I was enjoying a delicious meal, his companions having long since disappeared into the depths of the swamp.

Some friends!
They didn't even try to fight me to save their buddy.
What a shame, really!
I could have gone for some dessert...

DAY 2

Even if yesterday's dinner perked me up a little, it did not change the fact that I was still only a slime. Everything that surrounded me kept reminding me of that. The water in the swamp was truly a sea of mirrors, so wherever I went, I caught sight of my reflection and remembered just how ugly I was. I wasn't as ugly as a human—but still, I wasn't far off.

The big problem with eating Minecraftians is that it makes a mess everywhere. There's way too much leftover packaging!

You have to bite through the outer layer of clothing they've put on before you can munch on the interesting parts.

Looking at the remains of the human I had just devoured, I had a thought. They always wore clothes and armor. I had never seen one without something covering his body. I had always thought that clothing was worn to protect humans in case of an attack, but... What if there was another reason? What if humans wore clothes to change their appearance? After all, I couldn't blame them: Minecraftians are disgusting to look at.

They don't even have pretty green skin. It made sense they'd want to hide all that horribleness underneath a layer of clothing in order to look a little better.

Once I'd had this thought, I couldn't get rid of it. If a Minecraftian could change what he looked like with the clever use of clothing, then a slime surely could. After all, we are the superior species. It's well-known that slimes are the most intelligent monsters in the world.

I shivered with excitement as I began to think about my very first outfit. I was going to become the premier clothing designer in Minecraftia. Slimes would come to me from every corner of the world and wait in line for hours to buy one of my designs.

But what (materials) should I use?

DAY 3

I HATE BEING A SLIME.
DID I ALREADY SAY THAT?

Yes? Well, now I hate being a slime even more. Do you want to know why? It's completely impossible to wear clothes!

I closely examined every stitch of the Minecraftian's clothing to try to understand how it had been made. I wasn't too proud to learn something from humans. Evidently, this one's armor had been made of leather, which was a huge mistake if he was looking to protect his skin. What a funny idea, to think that you could resist a slime attack with only a bit of leather to protect you!

Still, leather was a good starting place for my clothes, so, the first thing I needed to do was find a cow, which turned out to be harder than I expected.

Usually, you find tons of these boring creatures just wandering around. We pass the time by jumping on them. But, when I most needed a cow, I couldn't find one anywhere.

I hopped about looking for what felt like hours, but it was actually only about five minutes. I was never very patient when I was excited about something. Finally, I heard the telltale sound of mooing. I rushed toward the sound and found a cow, stranded on a little island surrounded by swampy water. It was calling for help. What a shame for the cow that I was the first to arrive!

"Here, little cowy-cow," I cackled, as I charged at it and knocked it into the water.

"MOO!"

The cow let out a desperate call to its herd for help but it didn't stand a chance, and soon I had a superb piece of leather ready to be turned into a high-fashion garment.

And that's where I ran into my first problem. You see, Minecraftians have these strange appendages sticking out of their bodies. They call them arms and legs. Thanks to them, clothes stay in place. But we slimes . . . we don't have any arms and legs. We're nothing but big slippery blocks. It was hard to figure out where to even start thinking about a way around this.

I tried to drape the leather around me, to give myself some kind of shape and to create the illusion of a more interesting silhouette, but the leather kept slipping off me. The worst thing was, the more the leather brushed against my body, the stickier it became, and that made it harder to work with. What started out as a beautiful, large piece of leather got smaller and smaller as it stuck to itself, until, I ended up throwing it away, an icky, slime-encrusted ball of leather.

"IT'S RUINED!"

I grimaced in disgust, frustrated that I was not able to create something fabulous without effort. The Minecraftians always made it look so easy.

Once, on a day I had been very hungry, I went to a village. I normally don't get so close to groups of humans. It's not that I'm afraid of them. It's just that I don't want to have to defend myself from attacks coming from all sides. However, at this particular time, I didn't really have a choice. No Minecraftian had wandered into the swamp in ages, and I was starving. The village was the nearest source of food I could find.

Wandering through the village, I passed in front of an armorer and saw him making armor. He seemed to just wave his arms around and, presto! One set of armor. To this day, I have no idea how he did it. But me, I didn't have arms to wave about, and, even if I did, something told me it wouldn't be nearly as easy for me to make armor. I would wind up making a potato, or something.

I was going to have to go back to square one.

DAY 4

Maybe the problem was that I didn't have enough material to work with. If I had several pieces of leather, I could sew them together, and use what I made to cover each side of my cube. Then, I could add little details, like pockets, in order to make my outfit a little more interesting. It would be amazing, once it was finished.

I got super excited again. Everything that the Minecraftians knew how to do, a slime could do better.

WHAT'S THAT YOU'RE SAYING? IF THAT'S THE CASE, THEN WHY DON'T YOU SEE SLIME CITIES EVERYWHERE?

It's not that we can't build them, it's that we don't want to. Why bother? The rain doesn't trouble us. We just soak up the moisture and become even more slippery. It's all the same to us whether it's cold or hot, so we don't need a shelter to regulate our body temperatures, and there's nothing more wonderful in the world than the feel of sunlight on our gooey bodies.

There's no point in building something just for the sake of it, but—mark my words—if a slime wanted to build a shelter, he could. And it would be the biggest and the most beautiful shelter in all

Minecraftia. Maybe I'll make that my next project, after I've proven a slime is capable of designing and wearing clothes and having style.

This time, I didn't have to hunt for long to find what I was looking for. I came across a little herd of cows trying to find a path through the swamp. Why these stupid creatures even come to the swamp in the first place, I have no idea. Cow hooves are not made to walk on swampy ground, but maybe the reeds that grow here taste better than ordinary grass, or something like that. It's the only explanation I can think of. Otherwise, I don't see why cows come all the way here. It's either that, or they're even sillier than they look.

When I pounced on the first cow, the other cows scattered, but they were so stupid that they didn't know where to run, and they kept bumping into each other and slipping in the water. Meanwhile, I moved forward, slowly but surely, in their direction. It didn't take me long to collect a pile of leather, and I even snacked on some beef as I went, which was a nice little bonus.

Cow is not nearly as tasty as Minecraftian, but it does the trick when you get a little hungry after a long day of hunting. As I gathered up pieces of leather, I had an idea. A brilliant idea. The most brilliant and awesome idea in all of Minecraftian history.

Why was I trying to make ordinary clothes when I could make something extraordinary? Why didn't I create a DISGUISE?

If I looked like a cow, then it would be even easier to get leather. I could blend in with a herd and no one would notice me until—BAM!—I jumped on them.

And if I could trick the world by dressing up as a cow, imagine what I could do if I were disguised as a Minecraftian...

DAY 5

I was glad to have collected a big pile of leather, because making a cow costume turned out to be a big headache. There was a bunch of unforeseen complications—such as legs.

LEGS!

WHAT IDIOT THOUGHT IT WOULD BE A GOOD IDEA TO PUT LEGS UNDER A COW?

I managed to slap together some legs by rolling the leather up in a tube, and then tying the top of the tube with a bit of string, which I had made from vines. The legs didn't look too bad, but the problem was how on earth was I supposed to move with them?

I was able to tie the legs more or less together, but the hardest part was attaching the legs to me. I finally figured out how to loop the string around my body so that the tubes stood upright and I was perched on top. Then I encountered an even greater difficulty:

(How) was I supposed to walk with these things?

Slimes are not used to moving around on legs. I always thought jumping was a ridiculous way to move around, but now that I've experienced legs, I think jumping is, in fact, the most practical way to get from one place to another. You don't have to coordinate your legs or remember which one you just moved to make sure you don't fall flat on your face when you try to move forward. This is, if you could even figure out how to raise one corner of your body to move the leg forward.

Finally, I came up with a system that worked, but now I had yet another problem. How was I supposed to put the "body" of my disguise over the legs and attach the head to the front?

I struggled to figure it out, by myself, for ages. So many times, I wanted to drop everything and throw it all in the bottom of the swamp—but I refused to give up. I was determined to introduce fashion to my fellow slimes, and to prove to the whole world that slimes could look good.

I finished as the sun was setting. At last, I had something that more or less resembled a cow costume for a slime.

Tomorrow, I am going to do a test run and see if I can get close to a cow without being discovered.

DAY 6

It rained all night. Normally, that wouldn't be a problem, but it turns out that costumes made of cow leather shrink when they get wet. So, I had to struggle to put it on the next morning. You'd think slimes would be able to change their shape, huh, given that we're all wobbly and gooey. But no.

WE'RE NOTHING BUT VERY, VERY STICKY BLOCKS THAT STAY THE SAME BASIC CUBE SHAPE NO MATTER WHAT HAPPENS.

I put myself through a lot of pain, trying not to breathe and to make myself as small as possible so I could slip into my cow costume. It was a tight fit, but I managed to get it on. Really, really hoping that the string keeping everything together wouldn't break, I threw one front leg forward . . . and crashed to the ground.

"HA, HA, HA, HA, HA, HA, HA!"

I rolled onto my back, struggling to get the cow legs off my face, and I saw Tiffin, the swamp witch, laughing at me.

"That's the most ridiculous thing I've ever seen," she cackled between bursts of laughter. "A slime wrapped in leather, like a sausage! What are you trying to do?"

"Nothing," I answered, annoyed.

Why did she have to show up now, of all times?

"That's funny, because I wouldn't say 'nothing,'" Tiffin replied. "In fact, I would say you are trying to look like an animal. A pig...No, a cow! Why would a slime try to pass for a cow?"

"No reason," I muttered, gathering up the remains of my costume.

"I bet you're trying to look better. Let's be honest, though. Even the ugliest cow would still be better looking than a slime!"

"THAT'S A LIE. TAKE THAT BACK RIGHT NOW!"

Furious, I threw myself at the witch. Normally, Tiffin would be no match for an enraged slime, but this time I forgot I was still wearing my cow costume, and I got tangled in the legs again.

"Thanks for making me laugh, Bert. I haven't had such fun in a long time," Tiffin said, chuckling as she skipped off into the swamp. I cursed myself for having been stupid enough to try to make a costume that required me to coordinate four different legs—when I wasn't even used to using one.

It was too much. I gave up on the cow costume—it was a bad plan. But it didn't mean that I didn't have other tricks up my sleeve.

DAY 7

Okay, the cow plan had been too ambitious.

But I had still learned a lot from the experience, and I realized I could disguise myself as something else, something much closer to my natural shape. Even if my goal in designing clothes had been to change my appearance, I realized that I had bitten off more than I could chew. If I created an outfit that worked with my shape, then I would have a solid base from which to make more elaborate creations later on. I only needed to make one piece of successful clothing to get my confidence back.

But what is that marvelous creature, I hear you ask?

It was really so simple I could have kicked

myself for not thinking of it sooner. That is...if I had any legs to kick with.

I WAS GOING TO DISGUISE MYSELF AS A SHEEP!

Think about it.
What is a sheep, if not a cube covered in wool?

It's true that sheep also have legs, but I told myself I could do without them if I used enough wool. The other sheep would be so impressed by my fleece they wouldn't even wonder why I jumped instead of walked—and, when they finally asked themselves that question, it would be too late.

It had been ages since I'd treated myself to a nice, juicy piece of mutton or lamb. It was time for me to sneak into the center of a flock.

Usually, I eat a sheep when one has wandered into the swamp, but, going by my experience in making the cow costume, one sheep would not be enough to provide all the wool I would need. It would take me forever to get my hands on enough wool if I only used the few sheep that came to the swamp. I was going to have to go where the sheep were.

I set out straight in the direction of the nearest farm, once again excited by the idea of making clothes. There wasn't a minute to lose. I was going to create the most incredible sheep costume that Minecraftia had ever seen, and, after that, I would be on my way to becoming the very first slime fashion designer.

DAY 8

I got to the farm at sunrise, but the sunrise wasn't the only thing I saw...

"A slime! Slime attack! Everyone to the southern wall! We're under attack!"

A huge smile appeared on my face when I heard the panicked shouts coming from the farm.

I BASKED IN THE CHAOS AND CONFUSION THAT MY PRESENCE CREATED FOR HUMANS.

The farmers had reinforced their fences since the last time I'd passed this way. It was understandable. I had eaten a few shepherds as well as half a flock of sheep. Poor creatures. They had been no match for a determined slime.

This fence was not much of a deterrent, though. I cleared it in one jump and found myself in the field on the other side. I had come to take care of some sheep, but, faced with the shepherd and his men, my instinct took over. Slimes are the natural enemies of Minecraftians, and these particular ones were clearly ripe for the picking. I couldn't pass up the chance to treat myself to a nice bit of human, since they were right in front of me.

One especially brave shepherd charged at me with an ax in his hand. I couldn't keep myself from laughing when I saw his face. He was trying his best to look big and scary, but the only thing I could think when I saw him was, "Fast food!" I quickly disarmed him by striking him in the chest. He fell to the ground, winded. Having knocked him down, I made sure he didn't get up. The other humans wisely ran away when they saw how easily I finished him off.

Normally, I would have tracked down all of them until not a single one remained, but, because I was on a mission, I stopped myself.

A SHEPHERD WAS ENOUGH FOR AN APPETIZER. I HAD SHEEP TO MASSACRE!

IT'S REALLY EASY TO KILL SHEEP. YOU JUMP ON THEM AND—POOF!—THEY DIE OF FRIGHT, DROPPNG ALL THEIR WOOL.

I stopped counting how many sheep I took care of this way. In the end, there was so much wool on the ground I couldn't carry it all with me.

HERE'S ANOTHER INCONVENIENT THING ABOUT BEING A SLIME: IF I HAD ARMS, I WOULD HAVE BEEN ABLE TO CARRY MUCH MORE WOOL.

I did, however, manage to stick quite a lot of wool onto my sticky skin and stuff a lot more in my mouth. It tasted pretty awful, all muddy and filled with straw, but sometimes you have to suffer for your art. I was determined to bring home as much wool as possible, in order to figure out the best way to use it to create fashions.

Once my outfit was ready, I would go back to the farm to test it out.

If I managed to get to the barn without anyone discovering me, **I WOULD BE SUPER PROUD OF MYSELF.**

DAY 9

Looking back, I wish I had thought to collect more wool of the same color. But I had been so excited I'd just grabbed everything in sight. So, now I had pink, orange, black, and gray wool—all the colors of the rainbow. I had little bits of each color, but not enough of a single color to make an entire costume.

I would have to do the best I could with what I had. After all, you could dye wool, and I was sure that if I rolled around in swamp water the wool would all become dirty-gray, and that would do the trick.

First, I tried to stick the wool onto my body, trusting my natural sliminess to hold it in place. But, I quickly realized this wasn't going to work. The wool slowly slipped down my side and ended up in a little puddle of goo on the ground.

I was going to have to make a frame to hold the wool in place. Once again, I decided to use vines. Thanks to my work on the cow costume, I had gotten pretty good at weaving—and the more of it I did, the better I became. Soon, I had a frame big enough to cover my whole cube.

Then, I began adding the wool. I slipped it through the weave and used a bit of my own goo to keep it in place. I spent the whole day on it. When I was done, I had something that looked a little bit like a sheep.

In fact, once I put it on, I looked a lot like a sheep!

I soaked the costume in swamp water to try to make it one color. It didn't work as well as I'd hoped. You could still see some of the original colors showing through, but I told myself that if I stayed in the shade of a tree, no one would notice until they were next to me. And, by then, it would be too late.

I slipped on my costume and headed toward the farm.

TOMORROW, THEY'RE GOING TO GET THE SURPRISE OF THEIR LIVES!

DAY 10

I HAD A GOOD LAUGH AS
I NEARED THE FARM.

Those idiot humans were working nonstop, trying to make their fences higher. As if that could keep a slime out!

To be honest, I wouldn't even need to jump it. I could punch a hole in it pretty easily. If they really wanted to keep me out, they should have put out a bunch of traps and also made sure armed guards were patrolling the fence night and day. But, I'd still find a way in.

I was about to charge the fence when I remembered I was supposed to be a sheep—and sheep don't break through fences. I couldn't jump, either. If the humans saw me, they'd know I wasn't really a sheep. I sighed. I'd have to take the long way around. I went back into the bushes before a Minecraftian could spot me. Then, I made my way along the fence until I found a section that didn't have any humans around. With one leap I landed on top of the fence. Another little hop, and I was on the other side.

HA! THESE DUMB HUMANS WITH THEIR DUMB FENCES!

I heard sheep on my right, so I followed the sound, eager to see if my disguise would fool them. I came upon a big flock frolicking in the sunshine, so I hopped over to join them.

THIS WAS GOING TO BE FUN!

I looked around, expecting to see lots of sheep happy to welcome a new member to their flock. But, instead, they all froze in fear and stared at me.

"An intruder," one of them brayed. **"AN INTRUDER!"**

"No, no," I hurried to reassure them. "I'm a

sheep, just like you. I have wool and everything!"

One sheep was braver than the others. She grabbed my costume with her teeth and tore it off in one quick motion, exposing the real me underneath.

"A SLIME!" all the sheep brayed before dashing off as quickly as their legs could carry them.

It wasn't fair. I had worked so hard on my disguise. I was so proud of it—and it still didn't work. And the worst thing: when that sheep pulled off my costume, she ripped it.

IT WAS RUINED.

I saw some wool scattered on the ground. It might even have been from the last time I attacked the farm. I decided to gather it up. Even if my test had been a failure, I still had high hopes for making something really special out of wool.

Maybe the problem with my sheep costume was that it had been too simple.

.

I needed to aim higher.

Higher than sheep and higher than cows.

I knew exactly what I was going to do this time around, and it was going to be great!

DAY 11

"Keep your eyes open and your swords at the ready. Slimes have already been spotted in this swamp."

I heard the voices coming toward me, but I stayed crouched in my hiding place. I had known they were heading my way for a while now. Their odor stank up the whole swamp. Minecraftians don't realize how much they reek. If only they didn't use so much of that horrible soap stuff. They should do what slimes do—never wash. We let our natural fluids ooze, and that keeps us in excellent health.

When the humans drew level with where I was hiding, I jumped on them.

"AAAAH!" they screamed and dropped their bags.

A couple of them ran away, but three others stood their ground, determined to fight. This was fine with me.

I charged the nearest Minecraftian, knocking him back with a mighty blow. One of the two remaining humans managed to hit me with his sword, but I made sure that was the last time he ever struck me. I launched a series of attacks on him, forcing him backward until he tripped over a rock and fell into a pool of mud. I didn't stop, and he didn't get up again.

The two remaining Minecraftians circled around me, looking for their best chance to attack. I feinted to my right, and the human who was there jumped back to avoid me. The one on the left drew forward, but I hit him with such force that I knocked him out.

Soon, all three Minecraftians were down, and I was able to feast at my leisure. Though I would have loved to crunch on their bones, my main target, for once, was not the Minecraftians themselves. I had already gotten what I needed when I first attacked them. If these three humans had discovered my plans, they could have run away and lived to tell the tale.

It was their backpacks I was after and, when I rummaged through them, I found exactly what I'd been hoping for.

DAY 12

I was too excited to sleep, so I got up at dawn to begin my work.

I looked at the Minecraftian clothes I had spread out in front of me. I'd carefully pulled apart all the stitches to see how the different parts had been assembled, and laid them out flat in order to study the shapes.

I didn't know why I hadn't done this from the beginning, instead of trying to reinvent the wheel. I learned so much from the humans about how they made their clothes, and it wasn't what I'd expected. There were really so many different and easy ways to put together the separate pieces that, although I was a completely different shape than a Minecraftian, I still felt inspired by it all.

My next outfit was going to be a game changer.

DAY 13

ONCE AGAIN, I'D BEEN UP SINCE DAWN, WORKING AWAY ON MY CREATION. I WAS ON FIRE!

I weaved, I sewed, I glued leather and wool and everything else I could find that I thought would make my outfit better.

My stomach was rumbling, but I ignored it. You have to suffer for your art—and I wasn't about to go hunting Minecraftians while I had this streak of inspiration. I didn't want to risk losing it.

"What are you making there, slime?"

Tiffin the witch came wandering over to stick her nose in my business, as usual. I was still annoyed at her, for making fun of my cow costume, so I pretended not to hear her. Instead I focused on a tricky bit of sewing.

"You're not making another stupid costume, are you?"

She stuck her head right in front of me to sniff at one of my seams, forcing me to stop working.

"You are!" she chuckled. "I don't know why you're trying so hard. You will never be anything except a block of goo."

"Get away from here, witch!" I growled at her.

"Now, now, mind your manners." she teased, but she wisely stepped back before I could attack her. I don't eat witches, as a general rule. They taste weird, and when you get rid of one witch, two more arrive to take her place, causing a whole bunch of problems in the slime community. Though Tiffin was annoying, she was our local witch and we were used to her little quirks. It would be a real pain if we had a new witch move in and had to train her on how we did things.

After a pause, Tiffin added, "You know, your outfit will be much better if you infuse the cloth with a potion."

"A potion?"

"Oh, yes. Many Minecraftians use enchantments to make their armor stronger. You could use a potion of strength on your outfit to make it stronger. What's more, it will give you extra protection, in case you are ever attacked."

"A potion of strength?"

THIS WASN'T A BAD IDEA, BUT I DIDN'T WANT THE WITCH TO SEE THAT I WAS INTRIGUED.

I wasn't going to flatter her ego. It was already big enough.

"Do you have to repeat everything I say?" sighed the witch. "Do you have a problem with your hearing, or what?"

I looked away and ignored her questions.

"In any case, if you finally decide that you want a potion of strength, I have a lot in stock. I would be more than happy to sell you one at an honest price. If you need me, you can find me in my hut."

Tiffin took off and left me to think about her offer. Perhaps a potion was what my clothes had been missing all along. After all my disasters with cow and sheep costumes, it was certainly worth a try.

DAY 14

I was up all night working on my latest creation and, at last, it was finished. I stood back to admire my handiwork. I had outdone myself, and was excited to try it on, but first I wanted to soak it in a potion of strength, as Tiffin had suggested. I didn't want to risk it tearing when I put it on.

I hopped to the witch's hut and knocked on the door.

"Ah, Slibertius!" Tiffin was happy to see me. "I was wondering when you'd stop by. I knew you wouldn't be able to resist one of my potions. They're the best in all of Minecraftia, you know."

Of course they were. Tiffin was always bragging about being the best at everything.

"JUST GIVE ME THE POTION ALREADY,"
I grumbled.

"Tsk, tsk, not so fast," she said, shaking her finger at me. "I told you I would sell you one. Did you think I'd change my mind overnight and just let you have it for free?"

"Well, yeah. I could always just take it if I really wanted to," I said, menacingly.

"Oh, really?" Tiffin tapped her foot, raised her eyebrows, and crossed her arms. "I'd like to see you try, goo-head! Don't forget you're in my house! You wouldn't stand a chance against my potions. Fine, maybe you could beat me in a fight—but, without me, you couldn't even tell my potions apart. You wouldn't want to wind up with a potion of weakness or a potion of harming, would you? The results would be very funny—but probably not what you'd want."

This witch was making a big mistake if she thought she could win against me, even with the help of all her potions—but she raised a good point. I had no idea which potion was in which bottle. I didn't want to risk ruining all my hard work by picking the wrong one.

"Fine. How much for a potion of strength?"

"For you?" The witch thought for a moment. "I'm running low on spider eyes. Bring me twenty, and you can have your potion."

"Twenty spider eyes!" I exclaimed. "It's going to take forever to collect them all."

"Very well, then. If you're going to start complaining, we can make it twenty-four," Tiffin said, shrugging her shoulders. "A spider has eight eyes, so you only need to catch three spiders. But be careful. I don't take damaged goods, so if they're not in perfect condition, I will send you back to fetch me twice as many."

"It's a deal," I sighed. "I will find you twenty-four spider eyes. But this potion better be effective—otherwise I'll be back. And no matter

how many potions you throw at me, I'll be
having witch for dinner."

DAY 15

SPIDERS. I HATE SPIDERS.

Why did the witch have to send me after the only thing in the world I try to avoid?

Just the thought of those horrible eight-legged creatures was enough to send shivers down my spine. Spiders are the natural enemies of slimes, and we'd come to an agreement where they stayed on their side of the swamp while we stayed on ours, so we didn't have to deal with each other. But now, I was going to have to plunge myself into the heart of spider territory, and the thought filled me with dread.

Still, a potion of strength would be the perfect finishing touch for my outfit, so if I needed twenty-four spider eyes to complete it, then

I would kill three, four... **HECK!** I would kill TEN spiders if I needed to, until I got everything the witch wanted.

Then, my costume would be done, and I could show it to the world.

DAY 16

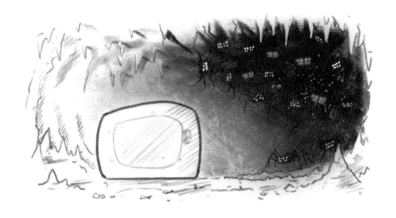

I hopped through the swamp, looking for spiderwebs. I made it to the darkest, coldest, nastiest part of the swamp, a place spiders loved and slimes avoided. The spiders' hairy legs were so revolting they gave me goosebumps, not to mention their huge eyes.

There was, however, one good thing about looking for spiders.

It made me realize there was one thing even uglier than a slime.

I was never going to make myself a spider costume. If I'd struggled with four legs, imagine what it must be like to coordinate eight legs.

YUCK!

I was so deep in thought, thinking about how ugly spiders were, that, without realizing it, I'd jumped smack into the middle of a spiderweb. The sticky threads stuck to my slime, and I had to dunk myself in the nearest puddle to wash it all off.

"Hey, you! You destroyed my web! I worked like crazy, spinning that!"

I looked up from the puddle and saw an angry spider scuttling toward me.

"And what are you doing on our side of the swamp, huh?" the spider demanded. "I thought we had a deal. You slimes, you have your own side. Go back there right now, before I make you."

I gulped. Facing one of these horrible spiders, all my childhood nightmares came rushing back. I used to wake up screaming from dreams filled with spiders attacking me. Slimes are strong, but so are spiders, and they know how to use each of their eight legs to their full potential.

Yet, I had come all the way here for spider eyes, and I knew full well that no one was going to just hand them to me. It was time to do what I'd come here to do. I took a deep breath, puffing myself up to look as big and menacing as possible, and threw myself at the spider, hoping that the element of surprise would give me the upper hand. If I could flip the spider onto its back, it would have a more difficult time fighting. Otherwise, it was going to be face-to-face combat, and that was going to be hard to win, even for an experienced slime like me.

I was about to strike the spider with all my might, when suddenly I felt myself soar through the air.

I'd been caught!

I'd landed right in the middle of a webbed trap, and now I was swinging from side to side, hanging from a tree in a spiderweb net.

I wanted to throw up, and not just because of the swinging. I'd been stupid enough to get caught by spiders—and now I was done for.

What had I been thinking? Was
it worth it, risking my life for some
dumb costume?

DAY 17

"Look how slippery he is! He's going to ooze right out of our trap if we leave him up there too long."

It was the following day. I pretended to be asleep so I could listen to the group of spiders talking about what they were planning to do with me. It wasn't going to be good, so the more information I could pick up, the better. I might learn something useful if they kept talking.

"Okay, slime. You can stop pretending. We know you're awake!" hissed one of the spiders.

I sighed and opened my eyes, wriggling about in the net so that I could look down on them.

"I HAVE A NAME, YOU KNOW!"
I cried in return.

"Do we look like we care?" the spider jeered.

"You're nothing but a slime, just like the rest of them. You don't need a name. You're nothing but a big useless glob of goo who should be banished from our swamp. This place would be much better without you and your kind in it."

"I could say the same about you," I replied. "You scuttle all over the place and destroy everything in your path. And your webs are real public nuisances. This place would be much neater without you and your kind."

"Those are very brave words for a slime caught in one of our webs," countered the spider. "Anyway, that's enough, no more joking around. Take him down and finish him off."

"WAIT!" I cried. "We should be able to come to some kind of agreement. I don't mean any harm."

"Oh, yeah?" chuckled the spider. "Then why have you come into our territory? You know you're not supposed to be here."

"I wanted some spider eyes," I muttered.

"Spider eyes?" the spider exclaimed in disbelief. "And how exactly were you going to get them without doing any of us any harm?"

"I said that I didn't want to harm anybody," I explained. "And that is the truth. But I need spider eyes to give to the witch."

"To the witch, you say?"

"Yes. I want to buy a potion of strength from her."

"She's selling you a potion?" asked the spider, suddenly looking thoughtful. "If she is selling you a potion, maybe she would be willing to sell us one, too."

I saw my chance, so I seized it.

"Why should you go all the way to the witch's hut? You'd have to cross slime territory to get there, and you'd be in the same kind of mess I'm in. You'd never stand a chance against all my friends. Why don't you let me go talk to the witch? I'm certain that I could convince her to give you a good deal."

"Or, why don't you buy a potion of poison from her, instead of your potion of strength?"

"But I don't want a potion of poison!"

"Maybe not. But we do. We're immune to poison but we thought it would be a lot of fun if we could spit poison on our enemies. One mouthful of potion, and the fight is over."

"WHAT AN AWESOME IDEA!"

I thought to myself, forgetting for a minute the trouble I was in.

I wish I'd thought of an idea like that.

Maybe I could build something into my costume that would allow me to spray potions on

Minecraftians. They would never see it coming.

"Thanks, we think so, too," said the spider, smiling widely. "We have lots of eyes to give the witch—so, if you bring us our poison, we'll forget you trespassed on our territory, and you'll be free to go."

I shook my head.

"Sorry, but I really need my potion of strength. Unless... If I bring you a potion of poison, would you give me eyes in exchange?"

The spider thought about it.

"That works," the spider finally said. "But it's in your best interest to return—otherwise we'll consider the pact between spiders and slimes broken. We'll invade your side of the swamp and we'll eliminate every slime that we come across, with or without poison."

I GULPED.

"Don't worry. You'll get your potion,"
I promised.

DAY 18

I arrived at Tiffin's hut the following morning and knocked on the door.

"Back already, slime?" she said, impressed. "I didn't expect to see you for a few days. Give me the spider eyes and I'll go get you your potion."

"Right, about that..." I began. "I don't actually have them yet."

"So why are you wasting my time?" Tiffin screeched, about to slam the door in my face. "Get out of here and go fetch me my spider eyes."

"NO, WAIT!"

I jumped forward to stop her from closing the door.

"I said I don't have the eyes yet," I explained, "but I can get them for you. I just need a potion of poison first."

"And you think that I'm going to just give you one for nothing?"

"It would be great if you did..."

I begged her with my eyes, hoping that she'd take pity on me and make my life easier. The witch threw back her head and shrieked with laughter.

"If I won't just give you a potion of strength, it's not likely I'll just hand over a potion of poison either, wouldn't you think?"

"That's true," I sighed. "What's your price?"

"I need more puffer fish," she declared. "Bring me five of them, and you can have your potion of poison."

"Five puffer fish," I repeated.

"You're not going to try to haggle again, right?"

the witch warned. "Because I can always raise that to ten."

"No, no," I hurried to reassure her. "Five puffer fish, very good."

"Wonderful. Now go away and stop bothering me. I have potions to prepare."

The witch slammed the door and I hopped off to the nearest lake.

DAY 19

I stared glumly at the puffer fish jumping out of the water, thinking to myself that all these little trips and early mornings were beginning to wear me out. That witch was really making me earn those potions.

Why couldn't she give me something simple to do?

Everyone knows that slimes and lake water don't mix. If I tried to go into the lake, I would dissolve. Catching puffer fish was not going to be easy. As I slumped down by the shore, I wondered how I'd managed to get myself into so much debt, not only with the witch, but with the spiders, too.

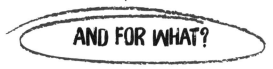
AND FOR WHAT?

If that potion didn't make my costume stronger, I would have my revenge on Tiffin.

I DIDN'T CARE IF THIS MEANT THAT THE FOREST COULD BE OVERRUN WITH WITCHES. TIFFIN WAS GOING TO FEEL MY WRATH.

But, for now, I was exhausted. I went home to get some sleep so I'd have enough energy to catch Tiffin's fish tomorrow.

DAY 20

New day, new energy!

I rushed to the edge of the lake to try and catch a puffer fish in mid-flight as it leapt out of the water. But they were too quick for me, and I had to make sure I wouldn't fall in.

I FELT DEFEATED.

I was there for hours, but I didn't catch a single fish. It wouldn't be much longer before the spiders became fed up with me and went straight to the witch themselves.

Suddenly, a delicious aroma tickled my nostrils. **A MINECRAFTIAN!**

It seemed like forever since I'd had a real meal, so I decided to take a break and give myself a little treat. Maybe I'd have better luck on a full stomach.

I went around the lake and spotted a fisherman with his line in the water. Even better! If I snacked on a fisherman, maybe, by osmosis, I would learn some things about catching puffer fish.

As I drew closer, I heard a snore. He was fast asleep! I just hoped he was having pleasant dreams, because this was one nap he was never going to wake up from.

I leapt on the villager, who was sleeping on his stomach, and began to devour him. If only puffer fish were as easy to catch as Minecraftians—then I would have gotten both potions by now.

At last I was full, and I sat back and looked at the lake. The fish were playing around in the water, as if taunting me with their every movement. I could almost hear them laughing, because they knew very well that I couldn't follow them into the lake.

"Come into the water and get us, slime!" they giggled.

I moved away from the fisherman and tripped over a basket overflowing with fish. It was the fisherman's catch of the day!

I was blown away by my luck. There was a ton of puffer fish in here, many more than I needed.

I hurried to gather them all up. I was closer than ever to getting my potion of strength.

DAY 21

The next day, I drummed on the door of the witch's hut.

"Delivery for Tiffin the witch!" I cried. When she opened the door, I placed the basket of fish at her feet.

"TA-DA!" I trumpeted. "Look! All the puffer fish you'll ever need!"

"Well, I'd be surprised if there were as many as that in here," Tiffin sniffed.

But I saw she was impressed. I had even packed a few fishing lures and other things I'd found lying around near the fisherman, just in case she would find them useful. I told myself it would be a good idea to be in a witch's good graces for the future. You never knew when you might need to ask her for a favor.

"So, can I have my potion of poison?" I asked.

"Well, I suppose so," Tiffin sighed. She disappeared into her hut and returned with a bottle filled with a strange-colored liquid.

"Here it is," she said. "Don't use it all at once. It's very strong."

"Don't worry, that won't happen," I promised.

Well, that wouldn't happen with me, anyway.

This potion was meant for the spiders, and it was their problem if they wasted it. Me, I only wanted my spider eyes.

DAY 22

I bounced across the swamp and couldn't wipe the grin off my face. I had managed to get a potion of poison from the witch without having to fight her, and now the spiders were going to give me their eyes.

Everything was going so much better than I had ever hoped it would.

"STOP! WHO GOES THERE?"

A spider jumped out at me, and I couldn't keep myself from recoiling. These things were so repulsive. Up close, they were even uglier than I remembered them being.

"What do you want, slime?" hissed the spider, who was clearly one their guards.

"It's me, Slibertius. I came here a few days ago

remember? I promised to bring you back a potion of poison—and here it is. So, if you'd like to take me to your spider leader—we had agreed on a bargain."

"A bargain?" the spider mocked. "We don't bargain with slimes. Thanks very much for delivering the potion. Give it to us and be on your way."

"No, no," I said, shaking my head. "We had a deal. You promised me twenty-four spider eyes in exchange for this potion, and I'm not giving you anything until I get what you owe me."

The spider burst into laughter.

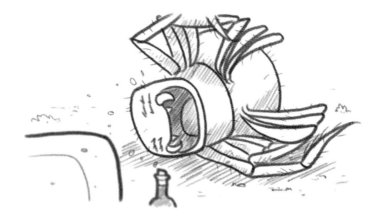

"We're supposed to give you what? Twenty-four eyes?" The spider convulsed with laugher and slapped his thighs.

"We will never give you any eyes. Whoever made you that offer tricked you. So, hand over the potion and be on your way. I won't say it again."

"I'm not giving you anything," I said. "If I have to collect my spider eyes by force, so be it. But, in that case, I keep this potion. I'm sure I can find a use for it."

"That potion belongs to us and you will give it here—or else we'll just take it."

"WE?"

It was my turn to laugh. The spider was all alone and I was angry enough to take it out on him without even thinking about it.

"You and what army?" I asked.

"Me, myself, and I!" jeered the spider. "Oh, and yes! My other friends as well!"

There was a rustling in the bushes. Three other spider guards emerged and took positions on either side of the first spider.

I gulped. One spider was bad enough—but four! These odds were not in my favor. But, despite everything, I refused to let them have my hard-won potion.

"LET THE BATTLE BEGIN!" I rumbled
and threw myself at the spiders.

They came to meet me head-on. This was going to be the battle of the century.

OW! One of the spiders bit me and I felt my goo tingle.

Oof! I took my revenge by hitting the spider smack in the middle of his eight eyes.

"THAT'S ENOUGH!"

The cry carried over the sounds of our fighting, and we all froze in place, tangled up with each other, desperately trying to cause as much harm as possible to our opponents. An enormous spider stomped through the clearing toward us.

"**GUARDS!** Would one of you care to explain to me exactly what is going on here?"

"I sent this slime on a mission," the larger spider, their leader, explained to him. "We are creatures who keep our word. What do you think would happen if we broke our promises? We are respectable monsters, not Minecraftians. You've tried to rob this slime? How dare you! Though he may be disgusting, we made a deal, and you should be ashamed of yourselves for having broken it. Apologize immediately."

"We're sorry," breathed the spiders before withdrawing, dragging their feet in shame.

"Now it is my turn to apologize," the spiders' leader continued as she turned toward me. "My guards ought to have shown better judgment. You can be sure they'll be punished for their actions. Please, have dinner with us tomorrow. Allow me to make amends for their bad behavior."

"With great pleasure."

Truth be told, I couldn't think of anything worse than eating with spiders, but I didn't want to risk offending the spiders' leader—not when I was so close to getting what I wanted.

DAY 23

"Isn't this magnificent? Our chef has really outdone himself today," Jiggly, the spiders' leader, exclaimed.

I fought hard to keep the disgust off my face as I looked at all the bugs spread out on the table in front of us.

I did not want to upset Jiggly, just as I was on the brink of getting what I wanted, but I thought I was going to vomit if I had to swallow even one of those creepy-crawlies.

"Go ahead, dig in!" Jiggly encouraged me, as she took a large mouthful of fried critters.

I took a deep breath and I closed my eyes, so I wouldn't have to look at what I was eating. I randomly grabbed something, tossed it in my mouth, and swallowed without even chewing, so that I couldn't taste it, whatever it was.

Curiously, it wasn't as bad as I had thought it would be. Still, I wasn't about to replace Minecraftians with bugs anytime soon. Finally, the feast came to an end. I had survived a meal with spiders, and I was probably the first slime in history who could say that.

Jiggly burped loudly.

"That was the best banquet in the world," she declared before turning to me. "What's the matter? You didn't enjoy your meal?"

"It was delicious," I assured her.

"So, why didn't you burp?"

"Oh, sorry."

I had no idea that spiders considered this to be good manners. Luckily, I've always been able to burp on command.

"I've been letting one simmer so that it can be loud enough to do justice to your hospitality," I added.

BURRRRRP!

I LET OUT THE BIGGEST BURP THAT THE SWAMP HAD EVER HEARD.

It was so loud it frightened birds out of the trees and fish out of the lakes.

It was so loud I even scared myself!

"Very good. Now it's time to talk business."

Jiggly led me to a part of the swamp I'd never been to before.

"We had promised you twenty spider eyes in exchange for the potion of poison?"

"TWENTY-FOUR," I corrected.

"Twenty-four," she laughed. "Of course."

The spider plunged her legs into the hole of a tree and brought out a little bag. She opened it and emptied the contents into one of her hands to count them.

"TWENTY-TWO . . . TWENTY-THREE . . . TWENTY-FOUR!" she announced, holding out the eyes to me. "Here you are. You can count them yourself if you wish."

"I trust you," I replied politely, pocketing my bounty.

"And our potion?" demanded Jiggly, holding out an insistent leg.

"Of course," I said. I took out the bottle the witch had given me and handed it to the spider. "Tiffin warned me that this mixture was especially powerful, and that you shouldn't have to use much of it."

Jiggly held up the bottle against the light. She was so busy marveling at how the liquid glittered and shimmered in the sun that she seemed to forget I was there.

"Now, we can conquer the world!" she exclaimed.

"MUAHAHAHAHAHAHAHAAAAAH!"

"Seriously?" I scorned, unable to stop myself.

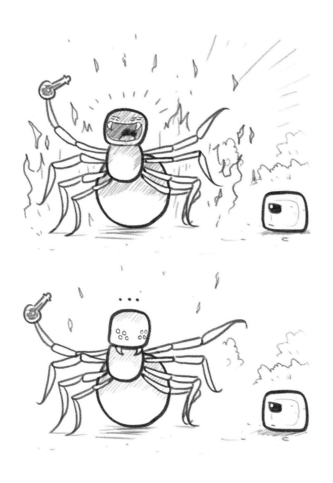

"Oh. You're still here, slime?"

Jiggly threw me a dark look and I understood that it was time for me to leave—before she decided she was tired of being nice to me and sent her guards to chase me. Whatever the spiders were thinking of doing wasn't my business. I had my eyes, and my outfit was so close to being finished I could practically taste it.

DAY 24

The next day, I was on my way to see Tiffin with the spider eyes in my hand.

I couldn't believe it.

I bet she had given me this task because she didn't think I could do it. I was looking forward to seeing her expression when I appeared on her doorstep to claim what she owed me.

I reached her hut and I knocked on the door.

"Tiffin! Tiffin! Open quick!"
Silence.

I went around the back, jumping to see through the window. No trace of Tiffin anywhere.

HOW FRUSTRATING!

I WANTED MY POTION RIGHT AWAY, DARN IT!

"AAAAH!"

Suddenly, Tiffin's scream tore through the swamp.

That wasn't good. Not good at all.

It sounded like it had come from the lake, so I leapt in the direction of the water as quickly as I could. When I arrived, I saw Tiffin surrounded by a band of Minecraftians. She was throwing potions at them as fast as she could move her arm, but she was outnumbered, and it wasn't going to take the humans long to stop her.

I couldn't let this happen. If they did away with Tiffin, I could kiss my potion goodbye.

"HOLD ON, TIFFIN! I'M COMING TO SAVE YOU!"

I plunged into the battle. The Minecraftians were so busy fighting Tiffin they didn't notice me until it was too late, when I was right in the middle of them.

"TAKE THAT!"

I shouted, as I sent a Minecraftian flying.

"What took you so long?" asked Tiffin, smiling, her energy buoyed by my arrival.

She pulled out another potion and hurled it at the nearest Minecraftian. While he tried to dry himself, I threw myself on him, knocking him out in a single blow.

I had enough food for weeks after all that!

"Thank you, Bert," Tiffin told me. "If you hadn't arrived in time, I don't know what would have happened."

"Here, let me give you a potion of strength, to thank you."

She rummaged in her robe and brought out the long-desired bottle. I couldn't believe it. On one hand, it was great to finally get my potion, but on the other...if I had known it was enough to run to Tiffin's rescue for her to give me a potion, I would have been happy to assemble a group of Minecraftians instead of going to pay the spiders a visit. This would have saved me a chunk of energy and time.

Oh, witches! I would never understand them not even if I lived to be a hundred years old.

DAY 25

I hid the spider eyes in a small hole, in case I ever needed them, and got back to my outfit. Because I hadn't looked at it for a while, I saw it with fresh eyes, and it was as wonderful as I had remembered.

I held the costume out in front of me: it was the perfect human disguise.

YES, I WAS GOING TO DRESS UP AS A MINECRAFTIAN!

I'd wasted a lot of time with the sheep and cows, when I should have been focusing my efforts on creating a Minecraftian outfit.

NO SLIME WANTS TO EAT SHEEP OR COWS WHEN THEY CAN HAVE HUMANS INSTEAD.

I uncorked the bottle and liberally soaked the fabric with the potion of strength. As the liquid was absorbed, the outfit seemed to shine, for a brief instant, with an eerie glow.

I pulled gently on the outfit at first, and then gave it a harder tug. It held! Using all my strength, I tried to rip the fabric—but it didn't tear. Tiffin was right. Her potions really worked! And this was exactly what my outfit needed.

I slipped it over my head and bounced toward the nearest puddle of water.

I stared at my reflection and loved what I saw. What an improvement on my basic slime look!

I WAS A GENIUS!

My creation was surely a turning point in slime history. We would never again be doomed to exist as nothing more than simple blocks. We could look however we wanted and be whatever we wanted. We could have fun blending into crowds of Minecraftians. They would suspect nothing—until we took off our disguises and devoured them!

The other slimes would be waiting in lines for hours to order my outfits.

I was going to make a fortune selling clothing. Not only was I going to change the course of slime history, I was going to become rich beyond my wildest dreams!

DAY 26

I put on my outfit. It fit me perfectly and it looked even better on me than it did lying on the ground. I was eager to see what the other slimes thought of it. I jumped to find my friend Phil. I could always trust Phil to cheer me up, and I knew he would be really excited about my costume.

"Phil! Hey, Phil!"

Phil was hopping around in the swamp, and, when he turned around, he did a double take.

"Bert, is that you in those rags?"

"These aren't rags, this is a Minecraftian costume," I corrected him, turning in a circle to show him the whole thing. "Tada!"

"I'M SORRY," HE SAID, WHEN HE'D FINALLY CALMED DOWN AGAIN. "I DIDN'T MEAN TO LAUGH—BUT YOU LOOK COMPLETELY RIDICULOUS!"

"NOT AT ALL!" I protested. "Look, this is the cutting edge of fashion. This time next year, all slimes will be wearing clothes like these."

"IS THIS A JOKE?" Phil asked, laughing harder. "Nobody will ever want to be seen in something like this! Anyway, slimes are perfect just the way we are. We're beautiful! You only need to look at yourself in the mirror to see it."

"You'll want one of my costumes," I insisted. "You'll see."

I hurried off across the swamp to find other slimes. Phil didn't know what he was talking about. The others were going to love my outfit.

"YOU LOOK STUPID!"

"DID YOU FIND THAT IN THE TRASH?"

"HOW LONG DID IT TAKE YOU TO PUT THAT GARBAGE TOGETHER? FIVE MINUTES?"

Everywhere I went, slimes kept making fun of me. I couldn't understand it.

Didn't they have any taste?
Or a sense of adventure?

Not a single slime liked my outfit. Still, I wasn't giving up hope. When they saw how much easier my disguise made it to hunt Minecraftians, they would change their minds.

DAY 27

I set out for the nearest village. I was going to prove to slimes that my costume was a brilliant idea.

Sniffing the air, I detected the scent of Minecraftians in the distance. There were two of them headed in my direction. Perfect! This would be the first test of my outfit. If I could trick these two humans, then I would be able to sneak into the village without anyone noticing me—and, once inside, I would be able to feast until my stomach was full to bursting. And then the other slimes would regret not coming with me.

The two Minecraftians walking toward me were getting closer, so I stretched myself out to look as tall and straight as possible.

I felt my pumpkin head wobbling and hoped the potion of strength would do its job and keep it in place. If my head fell off, I'd be so embarrassed.

"Hello there," said one of the humans.

"MMMMH!"

I had just discovered my first problem. I didn't speak Minecraftian! I could understand, more or less, what the humans were talking about, but I was unable to pronounce their words. I gave a little jump to make my pumpkin head nod, hoping this response would be enough for them.

The two Minecraftians looked at each other, confused.

"Okay, I guess," one of them finally said. "I think we're going to keep walking. Goodbye, whoever you are."

They took off at top speed, muttering and throwing looks over their shoulders. Either they were suspicious, or they had somewhere to be. In any case, they hadn't screamed, "A SLIME!" or drawn their swords, so I was going to consider this a success. I had shown that I could be close to Minecraftians without them attacking me.

My disguise was working.

Now, it was time to move on to the biggest challenge of all:

INFILTRATE A VILLAGE!

DAY 28

The following day I journeyed to the nearest village. I arrived at lunchtime and the village was busy—so it was going to be easy for me to blend into the crowd.

As I hopped toward the center of the village, everyone was looking at me sideways.

I didn't have any illusions. They were certainly talking about me behind my back, but I didn't care. The only thing that mattered was that they didn't suspect I was a slime.

The smell of Minecraftians was overwhelming. I did my best to restrain myself, because I wanted to explore the village. I hadn't set foot (in a manner of speaking) in a human city in a long time, and it was weird. There were buildings everywhere, filled with humans. I was spoiled with choices.

Should I snack on a shopkeeper or start off with a child as an appetizer?

Finally, I couldn't control myself any longer. It was time to unleash myself.

With a roar, I threw myself onto a villager... and fell flat on my face!

My costume was so comfortable I'd forgotten I was wearing it. It was impossible to fight in this thing!

I tried to tear it off, but the potion of strength had not worn off, and the fabric resisted all my attempts to tear it. Fighting to get the disguise off, I rolled around on the ground while a crowd of Minecraftians gathered around me, wondering what was going on.

"IS IT A ?"

a little child exclaimed.

"IT IS! IT IS A MONSTER! IT'S A SLIME!"

I hadn't even managed to get rid of my disguise yet, and my cover was already blown. It was a disaster! But, even worse, I couldn't defend myself because I was completely surrounded, and I heard the iron golems pounding toward me.

"TAKE THAT, SLIME!"

I felt the blow of a sword land on my back, and I yelled in pain. This was not at all how I thought my trip to the village would go.

Another sword struck me, and another, but just when I was on the point of giving up one of the swords cut through my outfit. I was free.

"AH-HA!"

I cried.

I leapt out of my suit, ready to jump onto the first Minecraftian who came my way—but, when I saw what was waiting for me, I paled. It looked like every armed Minecraftian in the world was in the village, and I was completely surrounded by swords pointed at me. I was wondering whether I would be able to run away if I jumped over their heads, when I heard an incredible commotion.

"Don't worry Bert. We're coming!"

The humans spun around to see a group of slimes, led by Phil, coming to my rescue. Some of the Minecraftians bravely stayed in place, but many dropped their weapons and ran for the nearest shelter, barricading the doors behind them.

"Phil, what are you doing here?"

Phil muscled his way through the crowd of Minecraftians to join me.

"I saw you heading out in your ridiculous outfit and I knew you were going to get yourself in trouble. And what are best friends for, if not to help each other out?"

"Thanks, Phil."

Together, we fought the Minecraftians until the slimes had conquered the village. Afterward, we wrapped up a few of the humans to snack on later and headed home. My costume may have been a failure, but, overall, the day had been a success.

DAY 29

*"So, what's your next outfit going to be?"
Phil asked me.*

"I've decided not to make them anymore," I replied. "It turns out to be a disaster every time. I've decided that being a slime is the best thing in the world. I don't know why I thought I could improve on perfection."

"Exactly. The cube is the building block of Minecraftia," Phil explained. "We're the best shape in the world."

It was true. Now that I had tried out different outfits, I had learned that the best thing was to simply and truly be yourself. A slime could not be improved.

We were the most awesome creatures in all Minecraftia.

"Since I'm not going to make any more clothes, do you want to go hunt some Minecraftians?" I asked Phil.

"Maybe later," Phil answered. "I still haven't finished digesting all the villagers we ate yesterday. I'm going to relax down by the lake, maybe even take a little nap."

"Sounds good. See you later!"

Phil hopped away. I was heading home to get some sleep myself, when I noticed something moving in the bushes. Could it be a Minecraftian who had come to get revenge? If so, how had they disguised their smell?

I jumped closer, and couldn't believe my eyes when I saw the bushes part to reveal a spider.

"JIGGLY!

WHAT ARE YOU DOING HERE? IF SLIMES FIND YOU YOU'RE GOING TO BE IN BIG TROUBLE."

"I know, but tell them that I'm here to do business and they'll let me go."

"To do business? What are you taking about?"

"The spiders heard about your outfits, and we think they sound fantastic. We'd like you to create Minecraftian disguises for us."

"*Minecraftian disguises?*

Are you serious?"

"Absolutely!" Jiggly said. "Only, figure out a way to include a mechanism that sprays poison. We tried spitting it—but there's something about spiders that makes the poison lose its powers once we put it into our mouths. So, we need a solution. We thought you would be the best one to invent something. We'll pay you for your trouble, of course. How do more spider eyes sound?"

"Spider eyes, you say?"

I thought about it for a minute. I thought about how I could buy all sorts of potions with the spider eyes the spiders would pay me with for creating outfits for them—the witch did seem to like those spider eyes.

"It's a deal," I finally said.

"I'll start by working on a sample. You'll have your Minecraftian outfits."

"Thank you."

Jiggly scuttled back to her side of the swamp, while the possibilities began to whirl in my head. If making an outfit for a slime had been difficult, it would be even harder to make one for a creature with eight legs—but I was ready for a bigger challenge. I didn't know why the spiders wanted their outfits, but I didn't care. I was going to become a famous fashion designer at last.

And if it wasn't fashion for slimes, oh well! I was still going to make a lot of money doing something that I loved—and that was all that mattered.

LOOK FOR:

ABOUT THE AUTHOR

Books Kid is convinced that behind every Minecraft character there is a story.

Early in 2015, he began writing his stories about Minecraft and publishing them as e-books on Amazon. He writes books to promote reading among kids, using the language of Minecraft that he and other fans of the game love. He has now penned more than forty stories, which have made it onto the list of the top 100 most-downloaded children's books.

But his dream truly became a reality once 404 éditions contacted him to publish his books in France.

ABOUT AYPIERRE

Since 2007, Aypierre has been creating fun and innovative videos about video games for his millions of followers. As a great fan of Minecraft, he fell instantly for the adventures of this slime.